This Rising Moon book belongs to

_____

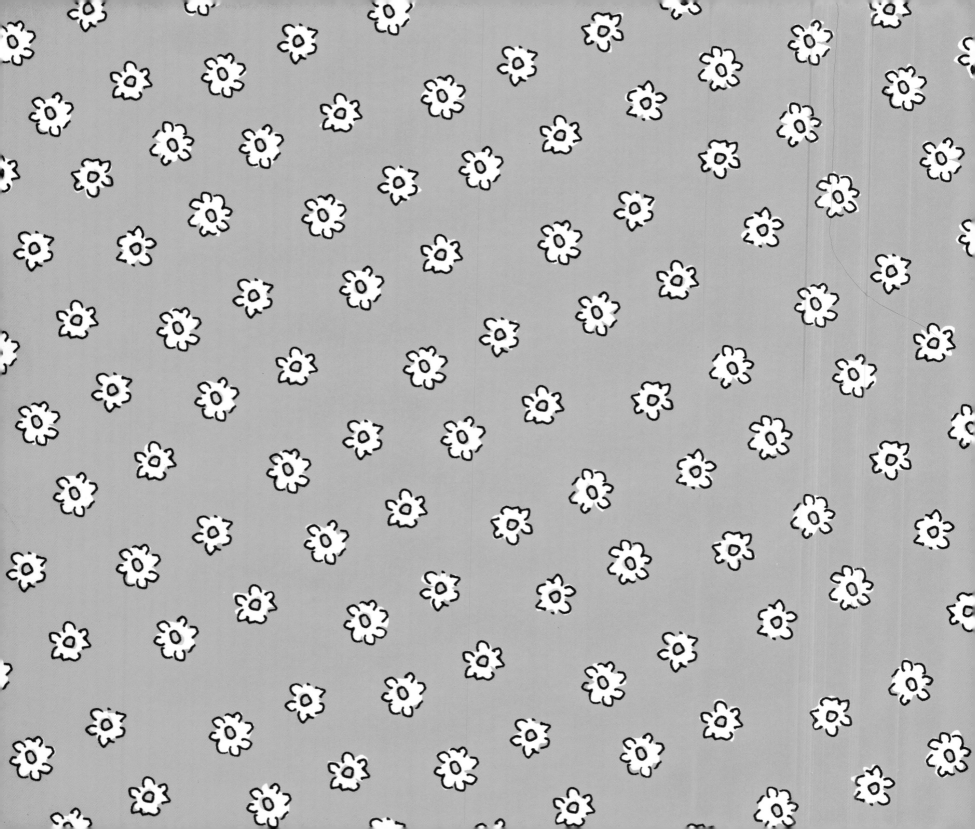

Do Princesses Really Kiss Frogs?

By Carmela LaVigna Coyle

Illustrated by Mike Gordon
and Carl Gordon

rising moon

www.risingmoonbooks.com

Composed in the United States of America
Printed in China

Edited by Theresa Howell
Designed by Katie Jennings
Production supervised by Donna Boyd

FIRST IMPRESSION 2005
ISBN 10: 0-87358-880-0
ISBN 13: 978-0-87358-880-5

07   08   09   5

Library of Congress Cataloging-in-Publication Data

Coyle, Carmela LaVigna.
Do princesses really kiss frogs? by Carmela LaVigna Coyle; illustrated by Mike Gordon.
p. cm.
Summary: A young girl takes a hike with her father,
asking many questions along the way about what princesses do.
[1. Hiking—Fiction. 2. Fathers and daughters—Fiction. 3. Princesses—Fiction.
4. Questions and answers—Fiction. 5. Stories in rhyme.] I. Gordon, Mike, ill. II. Title.
PZ8.3.C8396Dl 2005
[E]—dc22
2004016257

To my mom and dad
for their pioneer spirit!
— clvc

Daddy, what do princesses wear on a hike?

As long as it's sensible, they wear what they like!

How does she carry her water and snack?

She carries her things in her favorite backpack.

What does she see when she looks in the creek?

Hold my hand, and you take a peek.

Daddy, do princesses really kiss frogs?

They'd much rather kiss
their very own dogs.

Do princesses stop to smell the flowers?

They've been known to do that for hours.

What if a bee lands on the end of her nose?

The bee must have thought that her nose was a rose!

Will she meet a dragon when she comes 'round the bend?

Oh! That would be fun for us all to pretend.

Do princesses keep all the rocks that they find?

Maybe we'll ask if the ranger would mind.

Do princesses like to climb on the boulders?

I think you'd see better from the top of my shoulders.

What if a princess gets hungry and tired?

Then I'd say a treat and a rest are required.

Do princesses dangle their toes in the river?

If they don't mind getting a bit of a shiver!

Will princesses get to see rabbits and deer?

You never know what they might see and hear.

Daddy! Is that a REAL cowboy
hiking this way?

As real as this princess
with me today!

Oh Daddy, look at the view!

There's something about it that reminds me of you!

Place your
photo here.

A princess by nature...

Scavenger Hunt

The princess is going on a scavenger hunt! Can you help her find all the things listed below as she hikes through the book?

A moon

A butterfly

A fish

A ladybug

A spider

Footprints

A trail marker

A chipmunk

A bird's nest

A waterfall

Mushrooms

A rainbow

An ant

A bear

You can go on your own scavenger hunt, too. Before going on a walk with your family and friends, make your own checklist of things to look for. You never know what you might see and hear.